Kissing Coyotes

by Marcia Vaughan
illustrated by Kenneth J. Spengler

rising moon

www.risingmoonbooks.com

Composed in the United States of America
Printed in China

Edited by Rebecca Gómez and Theresa Howell
Design and Art direction by Dave Jenney
Production supervised by Donna Boyd

FIRST IMPRESSION 2007 softcover
ISBN 13: 978-0-87358-834-8
ISBN 10: 0-87358-834-7

Huizhou, Guangdong, PRC, China
Date of Production: Apr/13/2012
Cohort: Batch 1

Library of Congress Cataloging-in-Publication Data

Vaughan, Marcia K.
Kissing Coyotes / written by Marcia Vaughan ; illustrated by Kenneth J. Spengler
p. cm.
Summary: Jackrabbit brags to the other animals that he is so brave that he can do all kinds
of things, including kiss a coyote.
[1. Pride and vanity—Fiction. 2. Jackrabbits—Fiction. 3. Desert animals—Fiction.] I.
Spengler, Kenneth, ill. II. Title.

PZ7.V452 Ki 2002
[E]—dc21
2002031627

For Daniel Brower, the wacka-wacka man,
and an instrument of peace!

M.V.

To mom and dad
with much love and gratefulness

K.S.

Listen up now.

It all started down yonder at the watering hole when Jack Rabbit started doing what he did best.

Shooting off his big mouth.

"Roadrunner," said Jack Rabbit sitting back on his hairy heels. "You may think you're graceful, but I'm so gosh-darn graceful I can dance the *do-si-do* with a rattlesnake without getting bit!"

"Is that so?" replied Roadrunner.

"That's so!"

"Gila Monster,"
Jack Rabbit went on.
"You may think you're frightening as lightning, but
I'm so all-fired fearsome I can scare off a whole herd of
longhorn cattle easy as saying, *1, 2, 3, Ti Yi Yipee!*"

"That's a mite hard to believe," Gila Monster replied.

"Believe it!"

"And Fox," Jack Rabbit said, "you may think you're fast, but I'm so
fleet on my feet I can run right inside a skunk's burrow yelling,
Woo, woo, stinky-poo! and get away without getting
all stunk-up!"

Fox busted out laughing. "Jack Rabbit, you could talk the tail off a turkey vulture and never tell a lick of truth."

"You're all gurgle and no guts," Gila Monster agreed.

"You've never done one brave deed in your life," Roadrunner nodded.

Oh, that got Jack Rabbit so mad he thumped his feet in the dust. "Why I'm so rootin' tootin' brave I can kiss *all* the coyotes up on Tabletop Rock!"

"*Nobody* can kiss coyotes and live to tell the tale."

"I can," declared Jack Rabbit.

"Prove it!" all the animals said.

"I will," said Jack Rabbit. "I'll go kiss those coyotes right now."

It didn't take Jack Rabbit more than ten hops to realize what a plum dumb thing he'd done. He loped toward Tabletop Rock hoping there wouldn't be a coyote in sight.

Well, shucks, Jack Rabbit couldn't believe his bad luck. Yonder, dozin' in the dust, lay a he-coyote, a she-coyote, and a wee-coyote. Before he could change his mind, Jack Rabbit called up his courage. On quick, quiet feet he tip-toed timidly up and put a teeny tiny kiss on the tip of wee-coyote's paw.

K i s s.

And guess what? Wee-coyote didn't budge a bit!

Feeling a mite braver, Jack Rabbit snuck up to she-coyote and lay a kiss as light as a feather on the tip of her ear.
K i s s.
And guess what? She-coyote didn't notice at all!

Now Jack Rabbit was bursting with boldness. He strode over, puckered up, and planted a big juicy smootheroo smack-dab on the end of he-coyote's nose.

SMOOCH!

And guess what? He-coyote didn't twitch a whisker!

"Yee-haw!" Jack Rabbit hollered. "I kissed *all* the coyotes!"

And guess what?

WHOMP!

Jack Rabbit found himself squeezed tight as bark to a tree between two dusty paws.

"How Oww Owww!" howled he-coyote. "I caught a juicy Jack Rabbit!"

"He looks plum yummy," said she-coyote.

"Can I have the first bite?" drooled wee-coyote.

For once in his blabber-mouth life, Jack Rabbit couldn't think of a thing to say. He started quivering and shivering and shaking and quaking. His ears started flip-flapping like branches in a breeze. In no time, they were tickling the tip of he-coyote's nose.

"O w - c h o o - e e e!" he-coyote sneezed, letting his grip slip.

Without so much as a beg-your-pardon, Jack Rabbit lit out like lightning. He high-tailed it down the trail with that pack of coyotes hot on his hairy heels.

Dust swirled in the air as they chased Jack Rabbit up the ridge, down the ravine, and straight over Rattlesnake's rock.

HISSSSSSS-Spit.

Rattlesnake didn't like getting stomped on by Jack Rabbit's big kickers.

"Oh no, *do-si-do!*" yelped Jack Rabbit, dancing this a-way and that a-way, as he dodged Rattlesnake's bites.

That pack of coyotes didn't give up. They chased Jack Rabbit up the gulch, down the gully, and into the middle of a herd of longhorn cattle. All Jack Rabbit could think to say was, *"1, 2, 3, Ti Yi Yipeee!"*

That drove the longhorns loco! They stampeded right around Jack Rabbit and took off.

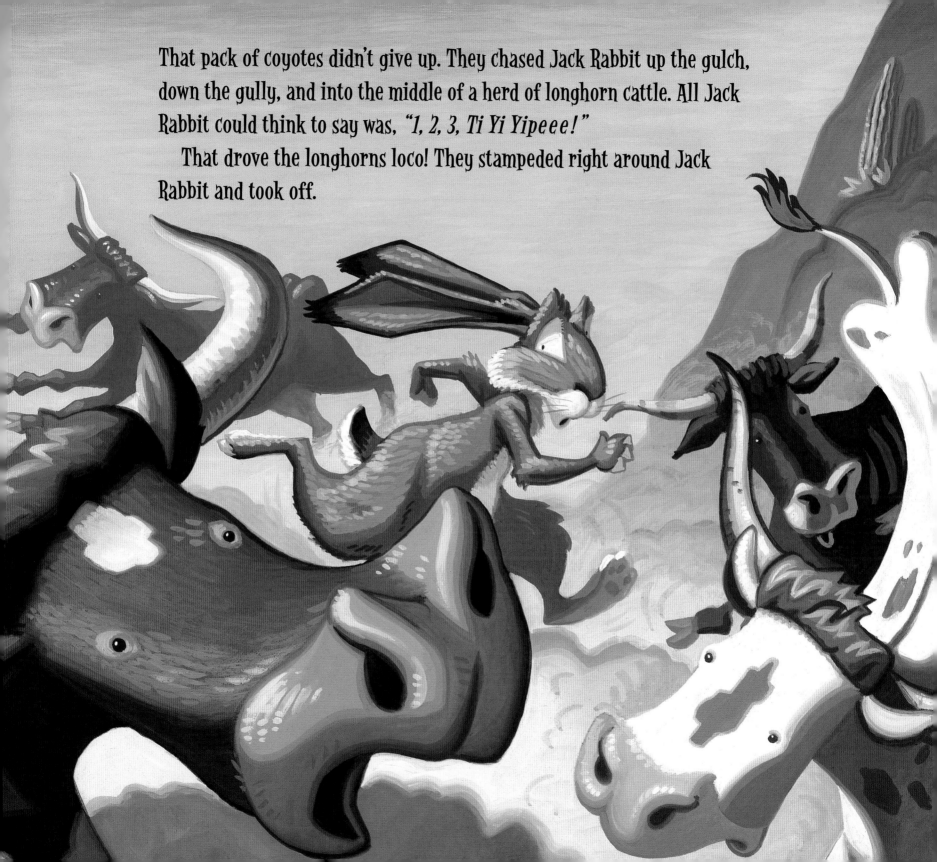

Now those coyotes were howling mad. They chased Jack Rabbit through the prickly pear patch, around the arroyo, and right down into the burrow of a spotted skunk.

"*Woo, woo, stinky-poo!*" cried Jack Rabbit, holding his nose in disgust.

Skunk didn't take kindly to name-calling. Flicking her tail high, she took aim and...PSSSSSSSSSST!

But Jack Rabbit was so scared and he was running so fast he simply skedaddled past that stink-awful smell.

That pack of coyotes didn't fare quite so well.

"Ew Ew Ew Pew!" they howled in horror. He-coyote, she-coyote, and wee-coyote ran lickety-splickety toward home as if a Texas tornado was on their tail.

Now that big-mouthed Jack Rabbit was all tuckered out. He shuffled back to the watering hole, his tongue hanging out like a rubber rope.

"Well?" asked Roadrunner.

"What happened?" wondered Gila Monster.

"Don't suppose you kissed any coyotes, did ya?" snickered Fox.

Jack Rabbit sat up and grinned. "Not only did I kiss those coyotes, I *do-si-doed* with a rattlesnake. I scared off a herd of longhorns shouting, *1, 2, 3, Ti Yi Yipee!* And I skedaddled past a skunk yelling, *Woo, woo, stinky-poo!* without getting all stunk-up! Now what do you think of that?"

Before Roadrunner, Gila Monster, and Fox could answer, Hawk came circling down from the sky.

"Howdy-do, Hawk!" cried Jack Rabbit, sitting back on his hairy heels. "You may think you're a fine flier, but I'm a far finer flier than you. I reckon I can leap off a ledge and glide above the desert without touching ground *all* night long!"

Hawk ruffled his feathers,
stuck his beak in Jack Rabbit's face,
and said, "Prove it!"

Marcia Vaughan has been a natural storyteller since her child-hood, when she used to sit on the back porch and tell wild sto-ries to her friends. Today she has written over 70 books for young readers. A former resident of Cave Creek, Arizona, she now lives in a lovely cabin on Vashon Island, Washington, where she plans on living happily ever after with her husband, son, and dog.

Kenneth J. Spengler began his career as an illustrator shortly after he graduated from Tyler School of Art with a B. F. A. His work can be found on anything from posters to billboards, and from mystery covers to children's books such as *Way Out in the Desert* and *Over in the Garden*, both from Rising Moon.

$7.95

rising moon
www.risingmoonbooks.com

ISBN 13: 978-0-87358-834-8
ISBN 10: 0-87358-834-7

00795

9 780873 588348